One of the most important ways children learn to read—and learn to *like* reading—is by being with readers. Every time you read aloud, read along, or listen to your child read, you are providing the support that she or he needs as an emerging reader.

Disney's First Readers were created to make that reading time fun for you and your child. Each book in this series features characters that most children already recognize from popular Disney films. The familiarity and appeal of these high-interest characters will draw emerging readers easily into the story and at the same time support basic literacy skills, such as understanding that print has meaning, connecting oral language to written language, and developing cueing systems. And because Disney's First Readers are highly visual, children have another tool to help in understanding the text. This makes early reading a comfortable, confident experience—exactly what emerging readers need to become successful, fluent readers.

Read to Your Child

Here are a few hints to make early reading enjoyable and educational:

★ Talk with children before reading. Let them see how much they already know about the Disney characters. If they are unfamiliar with the movie basis of a book, take a few minutes to look at the cover and some of the illustrations to establish a context. Talking is important, since oral language precedes and supports reading.

★ Run your finger along the text to show that the words carry the story. Let your child read along if she or he recognizes that there are repeated words or phrases.

★ Encourage questions. A child's questions are good clues to his or her comprehension or thinking strategies.

★ Be prepared to read the same book several times. Children will develop ease with the story and concepts, so that later they can concentrate on reading and language.

Let Your Child Read to You

You are your child's best audience, so encourage her or him to read aloud to you often. And:

★ If children ask about an unknown word, give it to them. Don't interrupt the flow of reading to have them sound it out. However, if children start to sound out a word, let them.

★ Praise all reading efforts warmly and often!

—Patricia Koppman
Past President
International Reading Association

For my "Beauty," Lauren
Hope, and the beauty
within us all   —G.T.

Pencils by Scott Tilley, Orlando De La Paz, Denise Shimabukoro

Printed in the United States of America.

3 5 7 9 10 8 6 4 2

Library of Congress Catalog Card Number: 96-85702

ISBN 0-7868-4072-2

The
Beast's Feast

by Gail Tuchman

Illustrated by Eric Binder
and Darren Hont

Disney's First Readers — Level 2
A Story from Disney's *Beauty and the Beast*

Disney
PRESS

New York

The Beast woke up
and out he flew.
"Tonight's my feast.
What should I do?"

The Beast called Lumiere,
who said to the Beast,
"I'll shine brightly
at your feast."

"Oh, good!" said the Beast.
"We'll have bright candlelight
at my feast tonight."

The Beast called Cogsworth,
who said to the Beast,
"I'll tick and chime
at your feast."

"Oh, good!" said the Beast.
"We'll have ticking and chiming,
and bright candlelight
at my feast tonight."

The Beast called Mrs. Potts,
who said to the Beast,
"I'll make hot tea
for your feast."

"Oh, good!" said the Beast.
"We'll have hot tea,
ticking and chiming,
and bright candlelight
at my feast tonight."

The Beast called Chip,
who said to the Beast,
"I'll blow bubbles
at your feast."

"Oh, good!" said the Beast.
"We'll have bubbly hot tea,
ticking and chiming,
and bright candlelight
at my feast tonight."

He called the others.
They said to the Beast,
"We'll come to your feast.
We'll dance and we'll sing.
We'll play and we'll ring."

"Oh, good!" said the Beast.
"We'll have dancing and singing,
playing and ringing,
bubbly hot tea,

ticking and chiming,
and bright candlelight
at my feast tonight."

The Beast went up and gave a shout,
"I hope these plans will all work out!"

"Hear that?" said Mrs. Potts.

"Start the fire.
Bring out the pots.
Wash the glasses.
Wipe off the spots.

"Shine the silver.
Roll out the rings.
Set the table
with all fine things."

And then out came the rest.
"We'll make it the best!

We'll shake.
And we'll bake.
Sweet treats
we'll all make!"

"Belle," said the Beast,
"Welcome to my feast!"

"We'll have treats to eat,
dancing and singing,
playing and ringing,
bubbly hot tea,
ticking and chiming,
and bright candlelight."

The Beast smiled at Belle,
who said to the Beast,
"What a wonderful night.
What a wonderful feast!"

"What a wonderful plan,"
thought the Beast,
"to have a fine feast . . .

for Beauty and
the Beast."